WHAT ROSE
DOESN'T KNOW

All inquiries should be addressed to:
Barron's Educational Series, Inc.
250 Wireless Boulevard
Hauppauge, NY 11788

International Standard Book Number 0-8120-1672-6

Library of Congress Catalog Card Number 93-36071

Library of Congress Cataloging-in-Publication Data

Foster, Kelli C.
   What Rose doesn't know / by Foster & Erickson ; illustrations by Kerri
Gifford.
      p.   cm. —(Get ready—get set—read!)
   Summary: When Rose closes the refrigerator door, the food inside talks
and moves around, but when she opens the door, everything "freezes."
   ISBN 0-8120-1672-6
   (1. Refrigerators—Fiction. 2. Stories in rhyme.) I. Erickson, Gina Clegg.
II. Gifford, Kerri, ill. III. Title. IV. Series: Erickson, Gina Clegg.
Get ready—get set—read!
PZ8.3.F813Wf   1994
(E)—dc20
                                                                                            93-36071
                                                                                                CIP
                                                                                                 AC

PRINTED IN HONG KONG
4567   9955   987654321

GET READY...GET SET...READ!

WHAT ROSE DOESN'T KNOW

by
Foster & Erickson

Illustrations by
Kerri Gifford

BARRON'S

"What do you suppose

goes on inside
when I close
the door?" said Rose.

When Rose closed the door

those inside awoke.

"Tell us a joke, Artichoke."

"Well," spoke Artichoke, "what is green and white and red all over?"

"Stop and pose!
Here comes Rose!"

Rose chose something to drink.

Rose closed the door
with a push and a poke.
Those inside then awoke.

"A light broke.
Look at the smoke.
It is making us choke!"

"Hold your nose. Find a hose."

"There is no hose, but I suppose,
we can stop the smoke."

Right away
they stopped the smoke.

"So, Artichoke, in your joke,
what is green and white
and red all over?"

"Me."

The End

The OKE Word Family

Artichoke
awoke
broke
choke
joke
poke
smoke
spoke

The OSE Word Family

chose
close
closed
hose
nose
pose
Rose
suppose
those

Sight Words

door
goes
hold
over
push
they
your
drink
light
right
inside
making
something

Dear Parents and Educators:

Welcome to *Get Ready...Get Set...Read!*

We've created these books to introduce children to the magic of reading.

Each story in the series is built around one or two word families. For example, *A Mop for Pop* uses the OP word family. Letters and letter blends are added to OP to form words such as TOP, LOP, and STOP. As you can see, once children are able to read OP, it is a simple task for them to read the entire word family. In addition to word families, we have used a limited number of "sight words." These are words found to occur with high frequency in books your child will soon be reading. Being able to identify sight words greatly increases reading skill.

You might find the steps outlined on the facing page useful in guiding your work with your beginning reader.

We had great fun creating these books, and great pleasure sharing them with our children. We hope *Get Ready...Get Set...Read!* helps make this first step in reading fun for you and your new reader.

Kelli C. Foster, PhD
Educational Psychologist

Gina Clegg Erickson, MA
Reading Specialist

Guidelines for Using *Get Ready...Get Set...Read!*

Step 1.   Read the story to your child.

Step 2.   Have your child read the Word Family list aloud several times.

Step 3.   Invent new words for the list. Print each new combination for your child to read. Remember, nonsense words can be used (*dat, kat, gat*).

Step 4.   Read the story *with* your child. He or she reads all of the Word Family words; you read the rest.

Step 5.   Have your child read the Sight Word list aloud several times.

Step 6.   Read the story *with* your child again. This time he or she reads the words from both lists; you read the rest.

Step 7.   Your child reads the entire book to you!

Titles in the
Get Ready...Get Set...Read! Series

Ages 4–7

The Best Pets Yet

Bub and Chub

The Bug Club

Find Nat

Frog Knows Best

A Mop for Pop

Pip and Kip

The Sled Surprise

Sometimes I Wish

The Tan Can

BRING-IT-ALL TOGETHER BOOKS

Bat's Surprise

What a Day for Flying!

Ages 5–8

Dwight and the Trilobite

Jake and the Snake

Jeepers Creepers

Tall and Small

A Valentine That Shines

What Rose Doesn't Know

Whiptail of Blackshale Trail